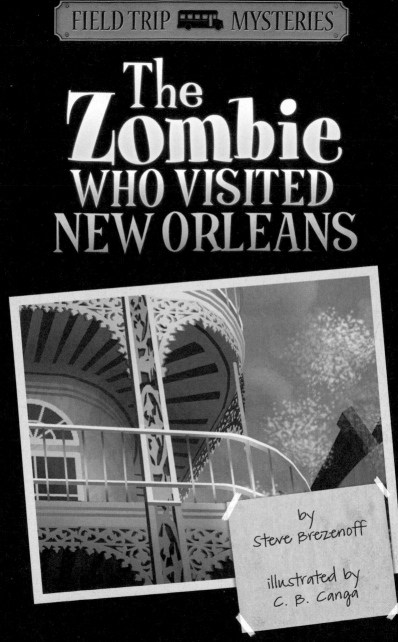

The Zombie
WHO VISITED
NEW ORLEANS

by
Steve Brezenoff

illustrated by
C. B. Canga

STONE ARCH BOOKS
a capstone imprint

r Samantha Archer,

Field Trip Mysteries are published by Stone Arch Books
A Capstone Imprint
151 Good Counsel Drive, P.O. Box 669
Mankato, Minnesota 56002
www.capstonepub.com

Library of Congress Cataloging-in-Publication Data is
available on the Library of Congress website.

Library binding: 978-1-4342-2141-4
Paperback: 978-1-4342-2773-7

Art Director/Graphic Designer:
Kay Fraser

Summary:
On a class trip to New Orleans,
Catalina "Cat" Duran and her friends
find themselves in the middle of a
voodoo mystery!

Printed in the United States of America in Stevens Point,
Wisconsin.
072011
006285R

TABLE OF CONTENTS

Catalina Duran

A.K.A: Cat

D.O.B: February 15th

POSITION: 6th Grade

INTERESTS:

Animals, being "green", field trips

KNOWN ASSOCIATES:

Archer, Samantha; Garrison, Edward; and Shoo, James. *Are these students spending too much time together?*

NOTES:

Catalina is well liked by most of her teachers and fellow students. *Sounds like a troublemaker.*

DOWN THE MISSISSIPPI

Our sixth-grade trip to New Orleans
was our craziest field trip ever.
New Orleans is an amazing city,
so it would've been cool no matter what.
But besides that,
there was magic,
mayhem, and monsters!

I should start at the beginning, I guess.

I've been on airplanes before, and on a train now and then. I've been in plenty of cars, and obviously lots and lots of buses. But I had never been on a riverboat.

It was amazing! This wasn't some old-fashioned paddle boat (I'll get to that later).

This thing was fast! The captain told us it was a high-speed riverboat called a hydrofoil. It actually went so fast that it left the surface of the river.

"This is so cool," Egg said. That's my friend Edward, but we call him Egg. He pulled his camera up and snapped a bunch of pictures. His camera is always hanging around his neck.

Gum blew a bubble and let it pop loudly, then went back to chewing.

I could smell that the gum was watermelon flavored. Gum's name is really James, but we call him Gum — not because he likes gum, though. It's a long story.

"Check it out. The Big Easy," Sam said. She's always saying weird stuff like that. In fact, she's the one who decided to call our friend Gum instead of James.

Egg and Gum and I looked at Sam.

"What's the Big Easy?" I asked.

Sam rolled her eyes and smiled at me. "It's the nickname of this city," she explained. "Don't you guys ever watch movies?"

We do, just not the ones Sam watches with her grandparents. They love old crime novels and detective movies. Sam sometimes talks funny because of it.

I'm Cat, by the way. But more about me later.

Finally, the boat stopped and the whole class headed onto the dock. A woman was standing there waiting for us. She was tall, and she was wearing a short white dress and a huge white hat. I guess it was to shade her from the sun. It was awfully hot. She was also carrying a white purse.

"Hello, y'all," she said. "Welcome to New Orleans!"

Our teacher, Mr. Spade, smiled and went over to her. "You must be Stella," he said.

She nodded. "That's right," she said. "I'll be your guide, every minute of every day, while you're here with us in Nawlins."

"What did she say?" Gum whispered to me, a little too loudly. I could smell that he had changed his gum from watermelon to root beer. As soon as one of his sticks of gum loses its flavor, Gum puts a new one in his mouth. He says he doesn't swallow the old gum, but I don't know if I believe him.

Mr. Spade turned and glared at Gum.

"Sorry," Gum said.

"That's all right," Stella said, laughing. "My accent must sound mighty thick to y'all. 'Nawlins' is how I say 'New Orleans.'"

"Ohhh," the whole class said.

"Now, let me show you to your hotel," Stella went on. She turned around and walked — it was more like a swish, really — down the dock. She only went about fifty yards, though, before she stopped.

"Here it is," she said. She smiled and put out her arms.

"Um," I said, raising my hand, "are we sleeping on the dock?"

Stella laughed again. "Of course not," she said. She turned to her left and threw her arms up again. We all turned too. We were looking at a huge, old boat.

I stared at my friends. They all looked as confused as I felt.

"You're staying in the Riverboat Hotel," Stella explained. "It was an old riverboat, but it's been turned into a hotel."

The Riverboat Hotel was nothing like the hydrofoil we'd been traveling in. This thing looked old. And I was pretty sure there was no way it could leave the surface of the river.

"Um," Egg said. He raised his hand. "Ma'am? Is it, you know . . . safe?"

Stella waved him off. "Sure it's safe," she said. "I'm on there all the time, and I haven't drowned yet."

She swished up the gangway. Mr. Spade followed her, so the four of us shrugged and followed them. The rest of the class came up behind us.

The ramp led up to a small deck at the front of the boat. Then there was a huge doorway to the inside. All around the boat were decks and railing and windows.

It kind of looked like a big old Victorian house on a raft. At the back of the boat was a huge paddle wheel. (See? I told you I'd get to that.)

"That wheel used to be how riverboats moved along," Stella said. "Y'all came down on a modern riverboat. They don't use paddle wheels anymore."

Stella led us inside the boat. It was set up just like any other hotel lobby. There was a desk, and a man in a black jacket with "Riverboat Hotel" in gold lettering on his chest.

"Hello, Stella," he said. He had the same accent Stella had. "Those copies you wanted are in." He patted a stack of papers on the desk.

"Thank you," Stella said sweetly.

Mr. Spade went up to the counter to check us in. Stella picked up the papers off the counter. Then she reached into her bag and pulled out two pins. She walked over to a corkboard on the wall and tacked up one of the papers.

"What's that say?" Egg asked me. The four of us were about to go check it out, when suddenly a door next to the corkboard swung open. A woman came sprinting out, screaming at the top of her lungs.

"Help! Help!" she shrieked. She dove behind the check-in counter.

"What's going on?" Stella said, shocked.

"Th-they're in the diner!" the woman replied.

"Who is?" Stella asked.

While the woman freaked out, Gum, Egg, Sam, and I snuck over to the swinging door. Above the door was a sign that read, "Ms. Pickle's Place."

We peeked through the window in the door. It was a small restaurant, with a counter and ten small tables. We spotted a big man in ripped clothing. He was facing the other way, and holding a big wooden chair over his head. Suddenly he threw the chair and it smashed through a window.

"Ahhh!" I shouted. I didn't mean to. But the man heard me, and he spun around so we could see his face. My friends and I gasped. Egg snapped a picture just before the man dived out the window, right into the river.

That was no man, I realized. That was a . . .

"A zombie!" the frightened woman said from the desk. "There's a zombie in my restaurant!"

"Zombie?" Sam repeated. "You must be crazy."

"Sam!" I said. "We saw him too!"

Sam shook her head. "Please," she said. "There's no such thing as zombies."

Mr. Spade and Stella tried to calm the woman down. My friends and I plopped onto a big couch along the wall. Suddenly, a boy appeared from behind a big plant next to the couch. He looked like he was our age, but he was a little skinny.

"I don't see what the big deal is," the boy said. "There are zombies all over Nawlins."

"Who are you?" Sam asked.

"Call me Dill," the boy said.

"Well, Dill," Gum said, "we think you're as crazy as that lady who just came shrieking through the lobby."

Dill shrugged. "I reckon," he said. "She's my mama. We own the café. And you can believe what you want. But people in this town know voodoo, and zombies are voodoo."

Sam almost laughed out loud, but she covered her mouth in time. "Voodoo?" she said. "Seriously?"

"Oh, it's very serious," Dill said.

Then Stella clapped her hands. "Kids, we're off to the French Quarter," she said.

"We have to go," I said. "Nice to meet you, Dill."

We got up, and Dill sat down on the couch. As we walked away, I looked back. Dill was shaking his head like we were making a big, big mistake.

The French Quarter is a section of New Orleans that the French built, obviously. It's full of old, beautiful buildings. There are fancy gardens, and long rows of two story buildings, with amazing iron verandahs. Also, even though it was still early in the afternoon, there was loud jazz and country and zydeco coming out of every store and restaurant.

During Hurricane Katrina, a lot of the French Quarter was underwater. Most of it had been rebuilt by the time our class visited.

Lots of people we met told us about how much their lives had changed because of the hurricane.

That day, people seemed to be having a good time. All of the restaurants were busy, even though it wasn't dinnertime yet. One restaurant had a poster for "New Orleans's Best Alligator." I shuddered, but Gum's face lit up. "I want to eat there!" he told me.

Our first stop was the Saint Louis Cathedral, the oldest cathedral in the country, built in 1789! We walked all over in the church. Stella pointed out lots of cool things. Then she gathered us together. "Legend says that one of the eighteenth-century men who worked on the church's design asked to be buried here," she said.

"Was he?" Sam asked. "Buried here, I mean."

"No one knows for sure," Stella said, a mysterious look on her face. "But if he was, I think it would be in this room!"

I shivered.

After our tour, Mr. Spade and our class followed Stella to a nearby gift shop.

"I better get something for my grandmother," Sam said. The four of us walked up and down the aisles. The shelves were packed with all kinds of crazy things, like alligator teeth and colorful hats.

"Hey, look at this," I said. I picked up a stuffed fabric doll. It had a crazy face and a feather stuck to its head.

"Cool, a voodoo doll!" Gum said. He grabbed it from me. "I'm buying this."

"Uh-oh," Egg said. "Do you have someone you want to curse?"

"Oh, not you too," Gum said, shaking his head. "Voodoo isn't real."

I chose an amazing Mardi Gras mask. Sam picked up a small wood model of an old-fashioned riverboat. It looked like our hotel. "Grandma will like this," she said. "Come on. Let's go."

The four of us went up to the counter. A man was sitting there on a stool, looking at his computer. He wore a red shirt and black pants, and had a big bushy beard.

"So, what do you know about voodoo?" Sam asked. She put the boat down on the counter.

The man hit a few buttons on his computer. "Voodoo?" he said. "That's a bunch of nonsense the locals like to scare people with. The boat will be eight dollars."

Sam handed him the cash.

"What about zombies?" Egg asked.

The man laughed. "Kids," he said, "it's all fake, okay? Zombies, curses, talismans, voodoo dolls. None of it is —"

We didn't get to hear the rest, because just after he gave Sam her change, he leaped off his stool and grabbed his butt.

"Oww!" he shouted. He ran from the counter, grabbing his butt and shouting. After running around the store, knocking over displays and screaming in pain, the man finally ran right out the door and into the street.

"Um," Gum said. "That was weird."

"I'll say," I agreed.

Sam shook her head. "Maybe his pants were too tight," she said.

The four of us headed out to the street too, but Egg grabbed my wrist. "Guys," he said, bending over to pick something up. "Look at this."

Egg held out a voodoo doll. It was obviously one of the ones they sold right there in the store, but it was dressed in a red shirt and black pants. And someone had glued a big, bushy beard onto its face.

Egg turned it over. Its butt was full of pins.

"Yup," Dill said, nodding. "That's voodoo."

We were back at the hotel. The four of us had told Dill everything that happened at the gift shop. We figured Dill seemed to be an expert, so maybe he could tell us something about it.

"I bet it was Anton Gutman," Gum said.

Anton is a boy in our class. He loves playing pranks. That's why he's always in trouble with Mr. Spade — not to mention every other teacher, and his parents, and the principal, and the woman who runs the pizza shop on River Road . . .

"The dolls were right there in the store," Gum said. "Anton probably stole it and some pins and had some fun."

"It wasn't any fun for the shop owner," I added. Gum nodded.

Sam clucked her tongue. "I don't know, Gum," she said. "Where'd Anton get the clothes? And the little beard?"

"They were probably for sale at the shop too," Gum said.

Sam raised her eyebrows. "That's possible," she said.

Dill laughed. "I doubt it," he said. "Not just anyone can practice voodoo."

"Maybe, but you don't know Anton Gutman," Egg said. "He's not the nicest guy. He loves pulling pranks and annoying everyone."

"Did someone say my name?" Anton asked from across the lobby. He walked over to us and we all hushed up quick.

"Hi, Anton," I said. "Enjoying the trip?"

"Oh, yeah," he said sarcastically. "I'm having a blast, Puppy."

His two goon friends laughed with him. They walked off toward the swinging door to the café.

"I guess it's supper time," I said to Dill. "We'll see you later."

At the café, workmen were repairing the broken window. While they worked, we had a good meal of burgers and fries. My burger was vegetarian, of course.

The grown-ups ate crawfish, a special Nawlins meal. I thought the crawfish looked like giant bugs.

The grown-ups talked a lot about Hurricane Katrina. Stella told Mr. Spade that it was the scariest thing she'd ever been through. But Ms. Pickle added, "But it really proved what a great city this is."

Stella nodded. "That's true," she said. "Everyone pulled together to help each other. It was amazing. Still is."

After dinner, Egg pulled out his camera and flipped through his pictures.

"This is sure a weird case," Sam said. "Zombies? Voodoo?"

"Spooky stuff," Egg agreed.

We all stopped talking when the waiter came over and started to pick up our dishes.

"Um, excuse me, sir," Egg said. "You have something on your neck."

The waiter reached up and felt his neck. There was a splotch of green just under his Adam's apple.

"Oh," he said with a shy smile, "must be from the broccoli soup I've been making. I'm the cook, too, and it's our special soup for lunch tomorrow."

Then he grabbed up our dishes and went into the kitchen. I thought he seemed embarrassed.

"Egg," I said. "You embarrassed him."

"Would it be better if I just let him walk around like that all night?" Egg replied. I shrugged.

"Back to the case," Gum said. "If you ask me, it's all very simple." He leaned back in his chair and blew a bubble. Then he said, "Anton Gutman."

"I don't know,"
I said. "Dill said
voodoo
is too complicated for
just anyone to do it."

"This isn't voodoo!" Gum said. "It's a couple of pranks. It's got Anton written all over it."

"What about the zombie?" I said. "That wasn't Anton."

"It was probably one of his goon friends," Sam said.

"But we saw its face, remember?" Egg reminded her. "I even took a photo!" He clicked through the pictures on his camera. "Look!"

It wasn't a great picture. It was obviously not a normal face — it was all melty and green and gross — but it was too blurry to tell much more than that.

"That could be a mask," Sam said. "There's no proof that it's a real face."

Just then Anton and his friends, a few tables away, laughed loudly. Then they went back to whispering to each other.

Sam shook her head. "I might be crazy," she said, "but I think I have to agree with Gum this time. It's all Anton."

CHAPTER FOUR

TAILING ANTON

Mr. Spade had already told us it was lights out. We were supposed to be in our rooms, sleeping. Instead, we were sneaking along the hall of the second floor of the Riverboat Hotel.

"Are you sure this is a good idea?" I asked.

"Trust me," Sam said. "How else will we discover what those three crooks are up to?"

"This is it," Gum said, stopping in front of a door. "Room seventeen, Anton and the goons."

"Shh," Sam said. "Let's keep quiet and hear what they say."

We stayed huddled, just outside the door, for a few minutes. I just kept thinking, *Please don't walk by now, Mr. Spade. Please!*

"Good thing none of our parents are on this trip," Gum whispered.

Sam nodded. "Or grandparents," she added.

Suddenly, we heard footsteps coming toward the door from inside the room. "Hide!" Sam snapped. "They're coming out!"

We darted around the nearest corner and peeked around.

"I hope they don't come this way," I said quietly. Sam nodded.

We were lucky. The three boys headed the other way, toward the stairs that went down to the lobby.

"We have to follow them," Sam said. "They must be up to something."

"Follow them?" Gum said. "Are you crazy? They left the door open. There must be so much evidence in there. We have to go check!"

Sam thought for a second. "Then we split up," she said. "Cat and Gum, snoop around in their room. See what you can find."

"Me?" I asked. "No way! I'm not going through Anton's stuff. It's not right."

Sam sighed. "Fine," she said. "Then you and Egg follow them. But hurry!"

"Let's go," Egg said. He grabbed my wrist, and we headed down the hallway.

Anton and his friends were already downstairs, so we had to move quickly.

We tiptoed down the steps into the lobby. All the lights were already off.

"Can you see anything?" I whispered.

"I can see the door to the café," Egg hissed back.

The small window in the door barely stood out against the darkness.

Suddenly, it moved. Someone was opening the door.

"They're going into the café," Egg said. "Let's go."

I'd seen enough, but I still went along with Egg. Better than staying alone in the dark lobby!

Egg and I pushed the door open. It creaked a little, but no one would have heard.

Anton and his friends were in the kitchen, and they were making a lot of noise. One little creak from the door wasn't going to get anyone's attention.

"What are they doing?" Egg said. "They're going to wake the whole hotel!"

"Let's just get some pictures and clear out of here," I replied. "I don't want to get caught."

Egg nodded, and we crept over to the café's counter. From there, Egg would be able to get a few good shots of Anton and his friends.

He raised the camera, aimed, and clicked. The flash went off. I tried not to scream.

Anton and his friends froze, then turned to face us.

"Oops,"
Egg said.
"Forgot to turn
the flash off."

Then a light came on above us.

"Who's in there?" a man's voice called out.

I held my breath.

"Run!" Egg said. We ran out through the swinging door and into the lobby. I nearly fell over the big plant next to the couch. We found the steps and sped upstairs to find Gum and Sam.

"Run!" Egg told them. We all raced back to our rooms: Sam and me in one, and Gum and Egg in the other.

"See you in the morning," I called to the boys. Then I closed our door and jumped into the bed.

Finally, I breathed.

CHAPTER FIVE

SOUP OF THE DAY

"I wonder what they were doing in there," Gum said.

We sat at our table at Ms. Pickle's Place, staring at the kitchen. We hadn't gotten a chance to discuss the night's excitement until we all met at breakfast. Dill had sat down with us too, so we filled him in on what Anton and his friends had been up to.

"You guys didn't find anything fishy in their room?" I asked.

Sam and Gum shook their heads. "Nothing," Sam said. "No zombie masks or voodoo dolls, anyway."

"Plenty of smelly socks, though," Gum added.

"I'll ask my mom if anything was missing from the kitchen when she opened this morning," Dill said. "She didn't mention the break-in."

"Well, it was a man's voice I heard," Cat said. "So maybe your mom doesn't even know it happened."

Dill shrugged. "Maybe I was wrong about your friend Anton," he said.

"He's not our friend," the four of us said together.

"Okay, okay," Dill said. "Well, whoever he is," he went on, "maybe he knows how to practice voodoo after all, and he was in here doing something."

The chef — the same man who had been our waiter the day before — came out of the kitchen.

"Maybe he turned on the light," Egg said, nodding toward the man. "Is that your father?"

Dill shook his head. "No, my father left town years ago," he said. "I was just a baby. That guy is Stella's boyfriend, I think. He hasn't been working here too long."

"Well," I said, "I hope he's a good cook. Because I am looking forward to the broccoli soup at lunch."

Dill looked at me like I was crazy. "Broccoli soup?" he repeated. "Today's Saturday. The soup is gumbo. It's always gumbo on Saturdays."

"Huh," I said. "Well, he's new. He probably made a mistake."

Sam frowned. "A mistake," she said. "Maybe."

CHAPTER SIX

SUSPECTS

After breakfast, Stella and Mr. Spade took us to our first stop of the day. I couldn't have been more excited. We went to the Audubon Nature Institute!

It was a dream come true for an animal lover like me. There was a zoo, an aquarium, an IMAX theater . . . even an insectarium! Have you ever heard of such a thing? I hadn't, and a lot of the class was grossed out. But I wasn't.

There are plenty of gorgeous insects, like butterflies and dragonflies and praying mantises.

Besides, even the gross ones are living things. I love all of them!

As the class walked from the insectarium to the aquarium, Anton came up behind us. He poked Egg in the shoulder.

"We know it was you," he said quietly.

"What are you talking about?" Egg asked. We all stopped and stood around Anton.

"You took a picture of me and the boys last night," Anton said. His good friends snuck up behind us, like they wanted to start a fight.

Suddenly Anton reached for Egg's camera. Gum grabbed Anton's wrist.

"Leave us alone," Gum said. "We didn't do anything to you."

"If that picture gets out, my friends and I will be in trouble," Anton said. "And we don't want that."

"Then maybe you shouldn't be bugging Ms. Pickle," I said, stepping in front of Anton.

"Yeah," Sam added, "not to mention the man at the gift shop yesterday."

Anton laughed. "The man at the gift shop?" he said. "What are you talking about?"

Mr. Spade came over before I could answer. "Everything okay over here?" he asked. "The rest of the class is already inside the aquarium."

"Sorry," I said. "We were just talking."

"Right," Sam added quickly. "About the . . . butterflies!"

"Okay, well, let's move along now," Mr. Spade said.

"By the way," our teacher added, "do any of you kids know anything about the missing gallon of vanilla ice cream, can of chocolate sauce, and jar of peanuts that went missing from Ms. Pickle's Place last night?"

My friends and I turned to Anton and glared. He just looked up at the ceiling, innocent as a newborn baby, and whistled.

SINKING

From the Audubon Nature Institute, we went straight to a go-kart course. Gum and Sam were super excited, but Egg and I were a little nervous. Those things went fast!

"We'll be wearing helmets," Sam said, trying to make us feel better.

"And seatbelts," Gum added.

"I'm sure it's safe," Egg said, but he didn't seem so sure himself.

Gum rubbed his hands together and grinned as we looked out over the course, and about twenty gleaming go-karts.

"Now we're talking," he said. "Nothing educational here. No bugs, or funny Latin names for sharks. No old churches. Just good quality fun."

While we waited for our cars, we talked about the case a little. We knew Anton wasn't doing any voodoo at the diner. Obviously he and his friends had stolen supplies for ice cream sundaes, and they probably had nothing to do with the zombies.

"So we're left with no suspects," Sam said. She sighed.

"Here we go!" Gum said. He was practically shouting. It was our turn to climb into some go-karts. Before I knew it, I was at the starting line, with Gum, Sam, and Egg around me — plus about ten other cars, all filled with our classmates.

The lights in front of us were red. Suddenly they turned orange, then yellow, then green. Everyone slammed on the gas pedals and squealed into action. Not me and Egg, though. We stayed close together, toward the back.

"If we stay away from everyone else," I shouted over the roar of the cars, "we won't get in an accident."

Egg nodded. "You got it," he said.

But the plan didn't work for long. Soon, the fastest drivers had made it around the track and were passing us! Before we knew it, Anton and his goon friends were passing us, laughing the whole way.

I'm sure Anton tried to knock Egg with his car. He definitely cut him off pretty close.

"What a jerk!"
I called over to Egg.
"That was really
dangerous!"

But Egg wasn't listening. His car was rolling to a stop. He was too busy watching Anton up ahead. I rolled to a stop behind Egg and watched too.

Anton was speeding into the next curve. He was going way too fast. If he didn't slow down soon, he'd definitely go right out of the course.

"Slow down!" I shouted. So did the woman who owned the course. She came running out of her booth, screaming at Anton to slow down. But it was too late. In an instant he crashed right through the plastic wall and flipped over onto the grass!

Everyone stopped their cars and got out. We all ran to Anton. He was already getting to his feet and pulling off his helmet.

"It wasn't my fault!" Anton shouted. He was very upset.

"You shouldn't have gone into that curve so fast!" the owner yelled at him. "We were all shouting at you to slow down. Goofing off is dangerous. You could've been killed!"

"It wasn't my fault, though," Anton said again. "Seriously. I wasn't goofing off at all. I tried to stop, but I couldn't."

"What do you mean, you couldn't stop?" I asked. "Didn't you hit the brakes?"

"Of course I did," Anton snapped at me. "But the brakes didn't work."

Suddenly he spun to face the owner. "We'll sue!" he shouted. "My parents will sue this place so bad, it'll never have another go-kart race again!"

"Come on, Anton," Gum said. "You're not even hurt. You don't have a scratch on you."

"I might have pulled my liver," Anton said, "or sprained my lymph nodes. Who knows!"

"How could this have happened?" the owner said. She put her face in her hands like she might cry.

Two men working for the course came over to examine Anton's car.

There, stuck to the bottom of the go-kart with some heavy tape, was a stick. It had feathers stuck to one end, and some weird paint all over it.

The two men looked shocked. The owner gasped. Stella looked so shocked I thought she might fall over.

"A bad luck talisman,"
she said. "Voodoo!"

"More voodoo!" Gum said.

Sam nodded. "Or something like it," she said. "It seems like every tourist place in town is under attack. And it obviously wasn't Anton this time."

"I wouldn't put it past him," Gum said.

"Come on, Gum," I said. "You think Anton would crash like that on purpose?"

Gum shrugged. "If his family really sues, they could buy their own go-kart course," Gum said. "Maybe Anton is very into go-karts, and he's always wanted his family to own a go-kart course. I bet he'd crash on purpose, just for the chance!"

We shook our heads. Poor Gum blames Anton for everything, and usually I think he's not so far off. But this time he was just being crazy.

"Dill!" Egg said suddenly. We all looked at him.

"Um," I said, "what about him?"

"Don't you see?" Egg said. "He knows so much about voodoo, right? And he was the only one in the hotel besides his mom and her chef before the zombie attacked. He has the know-how and the opportunity."

"Not bad, Egg," Sam said, "but you're missing one thing: motive. Why would he try to scare his own mom, or Anton, for that matter?"

"Well," Gum tried, "it's not like he was upset, even though his mother was cowering in fear behind the desk."

"True," Sam said. "Maybe we can find out a motive. Let's talk to him before lunch."

CHAPTER EIGHT

GUMBO ISN'T GREEN

We found Dill in Ms. Pickle's Place. His mother was wiping the counter, and Dill was pacing the floor, obviously angry.

"You can't sell the diner, Mom!" he shouted. "It's all we have."

"See?" Egg said quietly. "They're fighting. There's your motive."

Sam nodded.

When Dill's mom finally went into the kitchen, we surrounded him.

"Hi, Dill," Sam said. "So, why'd you do it?"

"Do what?" Dill asked, backing away. He bumped right into Gum.

"Why did you scare your mother with that zombie?" Gum said. "Why did you try to drown Anton?"

"And why did you freak out that gift shop owner?" Sam finished. "Fess up, Dill. This doesn't have to be difficult."

"Are you guys crazy?" Dill said. "I didn't do any of those things!"

"We noticed you didn't care much about the zombie attack," Egg said. "Everyone else was freaked out and afraid. But not you. Why?"

"I told you," Dill said. "There are zombies all over the place in this town. Everyone knows that."

"Come on," Sam said. "You don't expect us to believe this voodoo stuff is real, do you?"

"I promise!" Dill said. "For example, I saw one at the ice cream place down the pier. Just before the owner sold the place and left town, there were zombies there a couple of times."

"That couldn't have been good for business," Sam said.

"I don't know about business," Dill said. "But that ice cream man was very excited to leave town. He sold the shop to Stella really quickly. My mom said the price was way too low, too. But I guess he didn't care."

The chef came over. "Are you kids having lunch?" he asked.

We hadn't even noticed that the rest of
our class had come in and was sitting at
the tables. They'd already ordered their
lunches. The five of us sat down at a
nearby table.

"I'm going to have the soup," Sam said.
She winked at me.

"Okay," the chef said, smiling. "One
bowl of gumbo for the tall young lady."

"Gumbo?" Sam repeated, smiling. "I
thought you said it was cream of broccoli
today."

The chef's smile vanished. "I, um, must have been mistaken," he said.

"Then why did you have green on your neck?" Sam asked, but the chef didn't listen. He just turned and hurried into the kitchen.

"He didn't take our order!" Gum said.

I just smiled and nodded at Sam. I had a plan. Then I turned to Dill. "So, Dill," I said. "Where's this ice cream shop?"

THE CROOK, ON ICE

"You know, I was just going to suggest ice cream," Stella said as our class walked down the street. "I'm glad you kids thought of it. Ice cream will be just perfect for a lovely day like this."

"It's safe at the ice cream shop, right?" I asked.

Stella looked down at me as she walked. "Safe?" she said. "Why, whatever do you mean?"

"She means there are no zombies there," Egg explained. "Right?"

Stella threw her head back and laughed. "The old owner must have had some very powerful enemies," she said. "It takes a real master of voodoo to call for zombies."

"So I guess Dill's mom at the diner has powerful enemies too, huh?" Gum asked. He blew a bubble and it popped. Stella jumped.

I winked at Egg. It was time to act out our plan. He ran ahead a few steps and into the ice cream parlor, where it was much darker. As Stella walked in, he called out, "Say zombies!"

He snapped a picture. The flash went off, as bright as ever, and Stella was briefly blinded. Just then, Gum knocked into her shoulder, sending her purse — and everything in it — across the tile floor of the ice cream shop.

Everyone stopped behind us in the doorway, looking down at the mess on the floor. There was complete silence in the shop.

"Um," I said after a few moments. "I'll get it." I hurried forward.

"Oh, that's okay," Stella said. She tried to smile. "I can get it."

"Don't be silly!" Sam said, taking her arm. "Cat is happy to help."

I got down on the floor and
picked up a box of pins and a
tube of green makeup.
There was also a folded piece of paper.
I opened it up.

"Wow, what is all this stuff?" I asked.

Mr. Spade stepped into the middle of the shop. I handed him the paper. Mr. Spade looked at it for a few seconds.

"You're making an offer to buy the hotel diner?" Mr. Spade asked Stella.

"That's right," Stella said. "Ms. Pickle asked me if I wanted to, actually."

"This looks like a very low offer," Mr. Spade said. "You can't beat the location."

Stella shrugged and smiled nervously. "It's the best I can do," she said. "I'm not a rich woman."

"What are the pins for?" I asked, holding the box up.

"To hang up notices at the hotel," Stella said. "Ads for local businesses, of course."

"Mmhm," Sam said. "All your businesses, I bet, huh?"

Then Sam grabbed the tube of makeup from me. "And what about this?" she asked, spinning to face Stella.

"That's green makeup," Stella said. She reached for the tube, but Sam pulled it away quickly. "For a local performance of . . . um . . . *Frankenstein*."

"Right," Gum said, nodding. He stuck his head out the window. "Police!" he called.

"What are you doing?" Stella yelled, running to Gum and grabbing his shoulder. But it was too late.

A cop who had been walking nearby came into the ice cream shop. "Is everything all right in here?" the cop asked.

Mr. Spade looked at Egg, then at Sam, then at Gum, and then at me. I nodded at him.

"No, officer," Mr. Spade said. "It's not all right. I think this woman, Stella, is to blame for the trouble at the go-kart track this morning. She nearly killed one of my students."

"Is that right?" the cop asked. He stepped up to Stella and led her out of the shop.

"Wait!" Stella said. "You've got the wrong person! I — um — oh, whatever. You got me," we heard her say as the cop opened his car door and she got in.

"How did you kids know?" Mr. Spade asked.

Sam smiled. "It was obvious," she said.

"Once we knew Anton wasn't a suspect," I said, "we realized that the motive was more than just a prank."

"It was money," Egg said. "And Stella wanted more money."

"To get it," I explained, "she tried to scare the owners of the best tourist shops in the city."

Mr. Spade shook his head. "I still don't get it," he said. "Are you saying she knows voodoo?"

We laughed. "Of course not," I said. "But her boyfriend, the diner chef, is a big guy. And we saw some of the green makeup on his neck."

"Right," Sam said. "And she had all those pins in her bag."

"You mean she really used a voodoo doll on that gift shop owner?" Mr. Spade asked.

"Nope," I said. "But she did really use the pins. She must have planted them on his stool so they'd poke his butt. That way it would seem like someone had used a voodoo doll, and he'd get scared."

"Then once the shop owners were scared," Egg said, finishing the explanation, "they'd sell at whatever price Stella offered, just so they could leave town quickly."

"Dill's mom was pretty close to giving in," I added.

"Wait a minute," Anton said, stepping up to us. "Are you saying *Stella* almost killed me? It wasn't the go-kart course owner?"

We nodded.

"And she owns this ice cream shop?" he asked.

We nodded again.

"Score!" Anton said. "My parents will sue her! I've always wanted my own ice cream shop!"

Mr. Spade's eyebrows shot up. "You love ice cream, huh?" he asked Anton.

"I sure do," Anton said. "It's my favorite thing in the — oops."

"So, Anton," Mr. Spade said. "What do you know about some missing vanilla ice cream, chocolate sauce, and peanuts?"

My friends and I walked away. Mr. Spade could handle Anton. We'd already taken care of the real criminal.

literary news

MYSTERIOUS WRITER REVEALED!

Steve Brezenoff lives in St. Paul, Minnesota, with his wife, Beth, their son, Sam, and their small, smelly dog, Harry. Besides writing books, he enjoys playing video games, riding his bicycle, and helping middle-school students work on their writing skills. Steve's ideas almost always come to him in his dreams, so he does his best writing in his pajamas.

arts & entertainment

CALIFORNIA ARTIST IS KEY TO SOLVING MYSTERY – POLICE SAY

Early on, C. B. Canga's parents discovered that a piece of paper and some crayons worked wonders in taming the restless dragon. There was no turning back. In 2002 he received his BFA in Illustration from the Academy of Arts University in San Francisco. He works at the Academy of Arts as a drawing instructor. He lives in California with his wife, Robyn, and his three kids.

A Detective's Dictionary

accent (AK-sent)–the way a person pronounces words

dock (DOK)–a place where ships load and unload cargo

gangway (GANG-way)–a passageway leading to a ship

hurricane (HUR-uh-kane)–a violent storm with high winds

mayhem (MAY-hem)–a situation of confusion or violent destruction

motive (MOH-tiv)–a reason for doing something

opportunity (op-ur-TOO-nuh-tee)–a chance to do something

prank (PRANGK)–a playful or mischievous trick

suspect (SUHSS-pekt)–someone thought to be responsible for a crime

talisman (TAL-iz-muhn)–an object thought to have magical powers

voodoo (VOO-doo)–a religion that uses magic and spells

zombie (ZOM-bee)–in folklore, a person who is dead and has no soul but can move around

zydeco (ZY-dih-koh)–a kind of American dance music featuring accordion and guitar

Cat Duran

6th Grade

(A)

New Orleans

Monsters, magic, and mayhem. That's what we found on our trip to New Orleans. New Orleans is famous for being a magical city, although it usually doesn't have any monsters or mayhem!

When most people think of New Orleans, they think of Mardi Gras. Every year, the city is home to huge parades and parties. People come from all over the world to participate. Traditionally, Mardi Gras is celebrated the day before Ash Wednesday.

New Orleans is also known for being full of magic. The famous author Anne Rice, who writes books about vampires, makes her home there. Voodoo, a religion based on magic, is practiced by some people who live in New Orleans.

The biggest disaster to ever strike New Orleans was Hurricane Katrina in 2005. In late August, the category 5 hurricane approached the city. Most people had already evacuated, but thousands had not. More than 1,500 people died in Louisiana alone.

Over 80 percent of the city was flooded. Some areas are still not fully recovered. Many people say it was the worst disaster in U.S. history.

Now, the city continues to work on recovery efforts. Most people have been able to return to their homes, but some still have not. Through it all, the people of New Orleans became famous for their resilience, strength, and hard work.

Great job, Catalina. I'm glad you found so much inspiration in the people of New Orleans. Maybe next time you go, you'll try some crawfish! —Mr. S

FURTHER INVESTIGATIONS

CASE #FTM08CNO

1. In this book, my class went on a field trip to New Orleans. Where have you gone on a field trip? If you could go anywhere on a field trip, where would you go?

2. Why did Stella cause so many problems?

3. New Orleans was hit by Hurricane Katrina in 2005. Talk about that hurricane and other natural disasters.

IN YOUR OWN DETECTIVE'S NOTEBOOK . . .

1. The mystery in this book was solved by me and my best friends. Write about your best friend. What is she or he like?

2. Egg, Gum, Sam, and I met a kid named Dill on our field trip. Pretend to be one of us. Then write a letter to Dill, telling him about what happened when you returned home from the field trip.

3. This book is a mystery story. Write your own mystery story!

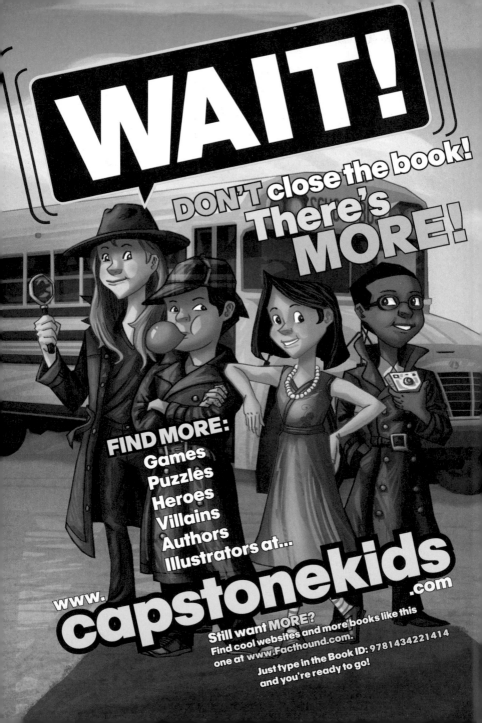